THE SLAVE

AN EROTIC ADVENTURE

VICTORIA RUSH

VOLUME 33

JADE'S EROTIC ADVENTURES - BOOK 33

COPYRIGHT

FEEL THE RUSH:

Jade's Erotic Adventures – Book 1

When lonely divorcée Jade seeks to broaden her horizons, she's invited to a private dinner event which promises to stimulate all of her senses. Wearing nothing but masquerade masks, dinner guests receive special service under the table while their fellow diners look on...

The Dinner Party

Jade's Erotic Adventures - Book 2

Jade discovers an exotic adventure club where strangers meet to explore each other's bodies in mysterious dark rooms. Using special effects to project swirling light patterns onto their figures, the shifting shadows provide just enough illumination to highlight their naked bodies while protecting their identities...

The Dark Room

Jade's Erotic Adventures - Book 3

Jade discovers a yoga club where members stretch and explore each other's bodies in the buff. She books an appointment, and during the first session meets a young redhead who tantalizes her with her flexibility and stunning body...

Naked Yoga

For the uninhibited...

1

———

I always looked forward to my weekly lunch date with my best friend and professional sex therapist, Hannah. But today, I had a different reason for wanting to see her. My sex life had become a bit staid and boring lately, and I wanted some new ideas for how to spice things up. As a newly liberated, polysexual woman, I'd had plenty of variety in my relationships, but I was tired of being the one always taking the lead seeking out new adventures. I wanted someone *else* to be in charge of plotting my sexual journey for a change.

I smiled when I saw Hannah waiting in the foyer of the trendy new Chicago restaurant, *Girl & the Goat*. Besides being my best friend and a font of sexual knowledge, she was super-hot, and my pussy tingled remembering our last tryst in the bushes behind the public library.

"Funny you chose *this* place for our meet-up this week," I said, kissing her gently on the cheek.

"How so?" she said. "I thought you'd like it, with its vegan menu and convenient location next to the 'el'.

"No, it's not that. It's the name: Girl & the Goat. Given

your profession and everything, it sounds like some kind of weird kink."

"Ha," Hannah chuckled. "It's certainly provocative, but I suspect it has more to do with the executive chef being a woman, and her proclivity toward farm-to-table food."

"Either way," I said, licking my lips. "As long as *you're* somewhere in the mix, I'm sure it will be super tasty."

After we sat down and ordered our entrees and some cocktails, Hannah rested her elbows on the table and leaned over toward me.

"What's up, girl?" she said, scrunching her eyebrows in concern. "You sounded a little down-in-the-dumps when I chatted with you last time over the phone."

"I dunno," I said. "I just feel like I'm in a bit of a rut. You know, *relationship*-wise."

"Are we talking about your *love* life or your *sex* life?" she said, smiling toward the waiter as he placed our drinks on the table.

"You know me," I laughed, taking a healthy swig of my margarita. "I'm still not ready for another long-term relationship after my last failed marriage. My sex life just feels kind of–predictable–lately."

Hannah suddenly hunched forward, coughing as she took a sip of her cosmopolitan.

"*Predictable?*" she said. "This coming from the girl who just came off a fling with the First Lady of the United States?!"

"That was a little different, I grant you. It's just that in most of my recent relationships, *I've* been the one taking the lead. I'm kind of getting tired having to take the first step and always being the one in charge in the bedroom department. Sometimes a girl just wants to be a lady, you know what I mean?"

"You mean being the *submissive* one for a change?" she said.

"I guess so. *You're* the sex therapist. Does there always have to be a top and a bottom, for want of a better expression, in every sexual relationship?"

Hannah paused while the waiter returned with our entrees, placing them in front of us on our place settings.

"That's the age-old question," she said, picking up one of her goat-cheese empanadas and chomping into it. "Traditionally, there's always been one dom and one submissive is most pair-bonds. I think it's a natural outgrowth of the old hunter-gatherer role of the male in a traditional heterosexual relationship and the homemaker/child-rearing role of the woman."

"Haven't we outgrown those old stereotypes in this modern enlightened age?" I said, shaking my head.

"You'd think so. But it seems to run deeper than that. Maybe it's a more visceral impulse, like with the alpha-beta-omega dynamic in a wolf pack. Whether they're hetero, gay, or lesbian, most couples naturally seem to assume one role or the other. With gays, it takes the form of 'tops' and 'bottoms' and with lesbians there's usually a 'butch' and a 'femme.'"

"But aren't these roles becoming more *fluid* these days with couples swapping positions from time to time?"

"Yes, of course," Hannah said, washing down her empanada with another gulp of her cosmo. "But each person seems to revert back eventually to their preferred position in the hierarchy. This seems like an odd question coming from such a sexually liberated person like yourself. It seems like you've tried just about *everything*. In fact, if I remember correctly, didn't you once avail yourself of the services of a professional dominatrix? Did you enjoy playing the submissive role in that situation?"

"Yes, but it all felt so manufactured, and temporary. Like I was *paying* to be dominated. It didn't feel natural."

Hannah shrugged her shoulders and chuckled.

"Well, you could pretty much walk into any lesbian bar in this town and find a dominant butch to take you on for a longer-term ride. With your pretty looks and that sexy body, you'd have no trouble picking up someone who's looking for some girly-girl fun."

"Mm, I don't know," I said, scrunching up my nose. "I'm not really attracted to that kind of woman. I guess I'm just looking for a 'normal' girl who I could experiment playing a more submissive role."

"What did you have in mind exactly?" Hannah said, leaning back in her chair.

"I don't know, someone pretty, kind of like *you*, who's not afraid to take the lead for a while..."

"Just how far did you want to take this whole submissive thing?" she said, arching an eyebrow.

"Whatever," I said, nibbling on one of my chickpea fritters. "I could go all-in, for a little while at least. It might be kind of fun, letting my partner have her way with me for a change."

"Hmm," Hannah purred, as a sly smile began to spread across her lips.

"*What?*" I said. "What are you thinking all of a sudden?"

"It's been a while since the two of us have had a roll in the hay, so to speak. Why don't we mix it up a little this time? I'll play the domme and you can be the submissive."

"That sounds like fun," I nodded, feeling my panties moistening at the thought of reconnecting with Hannah sexually. "But we've both had plenty of turns being the one on top–"

"No," she said. "I mean in a more *formal* type of domme and submissive role."

"You mean like in a BDSM type of thing?"

"Kind of," she smiled. "I was thinking more in terms of a *master-and-slave* type of role."

I lifted my hand to my mouth, suddenly coughing on a chick pea. Now it was *my* turn to be surprised.

"You want me to be your *slave*?" I said. "What would that entail, exactly?"

"Whatever I deem necessary," she smirked. "Whatever I want you to do, *whenever* and *wherever* we might find ourselves."

"You mean like in public places too?"

"Yes," Hannah nodded. "If the mood strikes me."

"That sounds kind of fun," I said, suddenly squirming in my chair at the thought of being at Hannah's behest whenever she demanded. "When did you want to start this little experiment?"

"How about right *now*?" Hannah said, peering at me with a devilish grin.

2

"Okay..." I said, suddenly intrigued. "What did you have in mind exactly?"

"I want you to get under the table and eat my pussy."

"Right *here*? Right *now*? There must be a hundred people in this place, and we're only separated by a few feet!"

Hannah peered at me as a slight curl formed in the corner of her lip.

"I'm going to get up and create a distraction. When you see the right opportunity, duck under the table. Nobody should notice with everything else that's going on. And the long table covering should disguise you while you're under there."

"What about when I need to get *out*?" I said, wrinkling my forehead in dismay.

"We'll figure that out when the time comes," Hannah said. "Now get ready. You won't have much time to make your move when the opportunity presents."

"Are you sure this is a good idea–" I said, peering around

me at all the restaurant patrons talking amongst themselves mere inches away from us.

"Don't worry your pretty little head about it," she said, rising from her chair. "This shouldn't take long. I'll be back in a flash."

Hannah picked up her purse and began walking toward the restaurant washroom. As she approached a waiter carrying a tray of food on his shoulder, she peered down into her purse, pretending to look for something. Suddenly, she tripped toward the waiter, and he stumbled, dropping the tray of food and beverages onto the floor with a noisy clatter.

"Oh my God!" Hannah cried, pretending to be just as surprised as the shaken waiter. "I'm so sorry. I was just looking for something in my purse–"

"Not to worry," the waiter said, bending down to pick up the fallen dishes and broken glasses on the floor. "These things happen more often than you can imagine around here. Are you alright? Did I spill anything on you?"

While the two of them continued their discussion, I glanced around me, and noticing that all eyes had turned temporarily toward the distraction on the other side of the restaurant, I flipped up the table covering and ducked underneath, feeling my heart pounding like a freight train.

I could hear Hannah and the waiter talking in the distance, then things slowly quieted down as the normal hum of chatter of the lunch guests talking and the kitchen staff working resumed. After a few minutes, Hannah returned to the table, placing her purse on the floor beside her and sitting down quietly in her chair. Fortunately for both of us, she'd chosen to wear a mid-length skirt today that provided ready access to her lower region while providing a modicum of cover from the surrounding restaurant guests.

Hannah slowly spread her legs apart and I could see in the dim light under the table a small wet spot in the middle of her sheer panties. Smiling at the ingenuity of her brilliant ruse, I reached under her skirt and threaded my thumbs under the top of her panties, slowly pulling them down to her ankles. I could see her bald pussy glistening from the moisture that had accumulated on her tumescent labia, and I paused for a moment admiring her pretty vulva.

"Ahem," Hannah coughed above me, strumming her fingers impatiently on the table.

Taking her cue to proceed, I spread her legs further apart and pressed my face between the gap, slowly licking the inside of her quivering thighs. Although I was nominally the submissive one in this unusual situation, that didn't mean I couldn't tease her for a bit and enjoy a certain degree of control while I followed her bidding.

As I moved my face closer to her steaming pussy, she shifted her hips forward, pressing her pubis toward my mouth. When I felt her wet slit touch my lips, I extended my tongue and slid it gently between her folds. Hannah groaned softly as she scrunched down lower in her chair, and I moved my hands under her skirt to grab the sides of her cheeks, pulling her harder into my face. As she slowly began to undulate her hips against my face, I raised my head, drawing a line upward between her dripping slit toward her exposed bulb. I could see it peeking out of its hood now, like a ripe cherry dangling on a tree.

Hannah flapped her thighs in and out around the sides of my head, and I could tell she was growing impatient for me to take her into my mouth. Realizing that we'd have a limited amount of time to consummate this act, I open my lips and sucked her gland into my mouth, rolling my tongue over her hardened shaft.

Hannah lurched forward and moaned as the dinnerware shook on the table above me. Feeling newly empowered tormenting her while the rest of the restaurant patrons went about their business oblivious to what was happening mere inches away, I snaked my right hand up between her thighs and thrust two fingers into her tight hole. She gripped the sides of the table with her two hands, trying to maintain her composure in the packed lunchroom. Suddenly, I heard some footsteps approach our table and the sound of our waiter's voice talking to Hannah.

"I see that you've finished your main course," he said. "Would you like something for dessert?"

Hannah peered up at him with glazed eyes.

"Oh, um—sure," she said, clamping my face between her legs trying to stop me from what I was doing while she spoke to the waiter.

"What do you have on offer?" she said, too distracted to look at the menu.

"Today's special is French silk pie or our signature Girl & the Goat cupcakes."

"The cupcakes sound fine, thank you," Hannah said.

"And for your *friend*?" the waiter said, peering at my half-finished plate of fritters. "Will she be rejoining you soon?"

I smiled as I listened to Hannah pretend like everything was normal while I continued curling my fingers inside her throbbing pussy toward her G-spot. She coughed as she jerked in her chair, trying to suppress the pleasure that was rapidly consuming her body.

"She just had to freshen up in the washroom," she said to the waiter. "I'm sure she'll join us again shortly. We'll order her dessert when she returns."

"As you wish," the waiter said. "I'll be back in a few minutes."

"Thank you," Hannah squeaked, her voice suddenly breaking from the feeling of my hands and fingers caressing her under the table.

When the waiter left, Hannah spread her legs further apart and she reached under the table, pulling my head toward her pussy firmly with one hand.

"You better get this over with fast," she whispered. "Before the waiter comes back and begins to wonder what happened to you. Besides, you're driving me crazy. I need to get off soon or I'll never be able to finish my meal."

Feeling just as eager to bring her to climax in full view of the other restaurant patrons, I stepped up the pace of my licking and sucking, drawing her button hard into my mouth.

"Yes, baby," Hannah purred. "Suck my pussy. I'm going to come in your mouth with everybody watching. You're being such a good little slave."

Hannah's dirty talk was turning me on almost as much as it must have been for her, and I squeezed her ass tightly imagining what it must have felt like to have someone licking your pussy surrounded by so many people. Her hips began to shake and I could hear her panting more rapidly above me over the table. I pushed my fingers harder up inside her, pressing my knuckles hard against her dripping slit while I flicked my tongue over her clit and curled my fingers against her G-spot.

Suddenly, Hannah grabbed the sides of my head with two hands and pulled my face tightly against her splayed legs as her hips buckled against my head. I could hear her groaning softly above me while she tried to suppress the waves of pleasure rolling over her as her pussy clamped down over my fingers in a series of powerful contractions. I held her nub in my mouth, feeling the walls of her pussy contracting around my fingers until her hips stopped quivering and her buttock muscles slowly relaxed. After giving her a moment to recover from her orgasm, I pulled my fingers out of her pussy and sat back on the heels of my feet under the table.

"What *now*?" I whispered to her through the draped tablecloth. "How am I going to get out of here now?"

"I don't know," Hannah said. "I don't think I can get away with another waiter distraction. Maybe you can just roll out of there pretending like you dropped something."

Hannah reached into her purse and tossed her compact onto the floor beside me. I picked it up and hesitated for a moment, then I flung the side of the tablecloth aside and rolled out from under the table, trying to appear as nonchalant as possible.

"I knew I'd dropped this thing *somewhere*," I said, holding up the compact to the startled guests sitting next to our table, then sitting down on my chair like nothing unusual had happened.

"Well *that* was invigorating," I said, smiling at Hannah as the lunch guests resumed their usual discourse.

"I'll say," she said, reaching down to pull up her panties. "I practically burst a gasket when the waiter came by at the worst possible moment. You weren't very helpful when you didn't take my cue to stop stimulating me while I pressed my thighs against your head."

"Oh *come on*," I said, smiling at her with a fiendish grin. "I couldn't let *you* be the only one having all the fun."

"Maybe so," she grinned, her face still flushed from the after-effects of her recent climax. "But it looks like I'm going to have to teach you a little more discipline about what it means to be a proper sex slave."

"Oh?" I said, raising a playful eyebrow. "What did you have in mind next for me?"

"You're going to have to wait until we finish our meal," she said, noticing the waiter approaching our table once again.

"Here are your cupcakes, ma'am," he said, placing a dish with two cupcakes on the placemat in front of her. Then he turned toward me, nodding toward my unfinished main course. "Were you finished with your entree, ma'am? Perhaps you'd like something for desert also?"

I paused for a moment, peering over at Hannah playfully while I glanced down at her plate.

"I'll have whatever *she's* having," I said, picking up one of her cupcakes and mashing it into my mouth as the icing dripped around the edges of my mouth.

3

———

After lunch, Hannah drove me back to her place, but she wouldn't tell me what she had in store for me next. When we pulled into her driveway, she led me out of the car and up her stairs into her master bathroom. Without saying a word, she turned on the large glass-enclosed shower and began to undress me. As the room began to fill with the warm mist from the running water, I looked over at her with a puzzled expression.

"What are you planning to do with me now?" I said. "Give me a golden shower?"

"That wasn't my intent," she said. "But now that you mention it, that's not a bad idea. No, I have some *other* dirty ideas in mind for you. But first I need to get us cleaned up in preparation for the next step in your education as a slave."

"Mmm, I like the sound of that," I smiled. "Are you coming in the shower with me?"

"Mm, hmm," Hannah nodded. "But don't get too excited. This is all about attending to *my* needs, not the other way around."

"That's okay," I said. "Just being in the shower naked with

you will satisfy my needs for the rest of the day."

After Hannah removed the rest of my clothes, she disrobed and the two of us stepped into the warm spray of the shower.

"Mmm, this is delightful," I said, sliding my naked body against hers as the water began to coat our slippery bodies.

"The first rule about being a slave is no *touching* unless otherwise instructed," she said, pushing me away. "Now pick up the bar of soap and give me a proper cleansing, and I mean *everywhere*."

"Okay..." I said, picking up the jasmine-scented bar of soap from the soap dish and beginning to rub it over Hannah's shoulders and tits.

"That's a good slave," she purred. "I want you to rub every square inch of me–and don't forget all the hidden crevasses."

"It'll be my pleasure," I said, ogling Hannah's glistening body under the bright light of the shower.

As instructed, I was careful to roll the soap over every part of her body, starting at the top and working my way downward. When I reached her mound, I felt the bar of soap sticking for a moment on the short stubble of her pubis, and the bar fell onto the floor.

"Sorry, Hannah," I said, bending down to retrieve the bar.

"That's okay," she said, peering at my upturned butt as I leaned over at the waist. "I kind of prefer you from this angle anyway. But from now on, I want you to refer to me as Master. I will refer to you simply as Slave."

Hannah slapped my ass hard from behind and I lurched forward, almost losing my footing on the slippery floor. Then she reached between my legs and clamped her hand around my upturned mound with a firm grip, pulling me toward her.

"Do you *like* it when I play rough with you, Slave?"

Mmm, yes, Master," I sputtered as the water streamed down my back and flowed over the front of my face.

Hannah slapped my other butt cheek hard before instructing me to resume my cleaning ritual.

"Now stand up and finish the job. You still haven't finished cleaning my lower regions."

"Yes, Master," I said, repositioning myself in front of her and rolling the bar of soap over her mound and between her legs toward her perineum.

"Yes," Hannah jerked, feeling the slippery bar sliding over her sensitive parts. "Just like that. I want you to give my private parts extra special attention."

"Yes, Master," I smiled, angling the bar between her folds and rubbing it softly over the base of her mound where her clit poked out, aroused by the combination of the slippery soap rubbing against her and the warm water streaming between her legs.

But just as I was getting into lavishing her pussy with the slippery bar, she turned around and tilted her ass up with her hands resting on the side of the shower wall.

"Now clean my pucker too," she instructed. "I want to feel you caressing *every* part of me."

"Mmm," I hummed, only too happy to touch the most private parts of her body.

I separated her butt cheeks, then slowly ran the bar of soap between her crack, caressing her rosebud with the tips of my fingers.

"Yes," she panted. "I like the touch of your fingers on my butthole. Now coat your fingers with some soap and insert two of them inside me."

"In your *anus*?" I said, shocked at the audacity of her invitation.

"Yes," she said. "Just a little way, up to the first knuckle or so. I want to see what it feels like to have you rim me with your fingers."

I rolled the bar of soap in my hands then pressed my forefinger and middle finger slowly into her sphincter, being careful to keep my nails pointed upward so as not to pinch her sensitive tissue.

"*Fuck* yes," Hannah hissed, pressing her ass back toward me to meet the pressure of my probing fingers. "Now curl them around in there a little bit like when you finger my pussy."

As I began to gently move my fingers around in her butt-hole, I was surprised how much of a turn-on it was for me. This was something I'd never really explored before, and there was something very sexy and raunchy about pegging my girlfriend from behind, even if it *was* just with the tips of my fingers. Her sphincter was tighter than I imagined, and I felt my pussy throbbing under the warm flow of water splashing over the two of us while I probed her from behind.

"That's enough," she suddenly said, tilting her hips forward and making a plopping sound as my fingers popped out of her hole. "Now wash your hands with the bar of soap and rinse the rest of my perineum before cleaning my legs and feet."

While I followed Hannah's instructions, I slowly bent down at my knees, moving further and further down her body until I reached her feet. She lifted up one foot then the other, giving me access to the bottom of her soles, then she grabbed my wet hair, pulling my face hard into her open pussy. I choked for a moment from the combined pressure of her wet flesh covering my nose and mouth and from the cascade of water pouring down over her stomach onto my upturned face. But instead of giving me a chance to continue licking and sucking her pussy as in the restaurant, after a few seconds she pulled my head back and peered down at me while I blinked up at her under the spray of falling water.

"That's a good slave," she smiled. "I think we're finished in here. Now get up and fetch me a towel to dry me off."

"Yes, Master," I said, disappointed that she wasn't going to give me a chance to finish the job I'd started.

I scrambled out of the shower and tip-toed over the wet floor to retrieve a bath towel from the towel rack, then Hannah stepped out of the shower and turned around while I patted her dry.

"That'll do," Hannah said, taking the towel from me and walking over to the padded stool in front of her make-up mirror. "Now I want you to attend to some personal grooming. Get on your knees on the floor while I gather the necessary tools."

What kind of tools did she have in mind? I thought. *She's really getting into this whole role-playing scenario.*

But it didn't bother me since I was actually enjoying this little role reversal and eager to see what she had in mind next. I bent down on the wet tile floor, wondering why she hadn't allowed me to towel myself dry, feeling the residual water from the shower dripping out of my hair down the middle of my back and over the crack of my ass. I shivered from the sensation, not because I was cold, but from the feeling of the warm water caressing my splayed labia and tingling clit, now fully exposed from my heightened state of arousal.

When Hannah returned, she placed a women's razor and a tube of shave gel on the floor beside me, then she sat down on the stool, spreading her legs wide in front of my face.

"It's been a while since I've shaved my pussy," she said. "It's getting a little rough down there. I want you to shave me nice and smooth, just like you are."

Hannah knew that I'd undergone laser treatment to remove every trace of hair from my perineum area, but she'd been holding off having similar treatment for fear of the pain involved in the procedure.

"And you better be careful not to cut or nick me down there, or there'll be severe consequences."

"Yes ma'am—er, *Master*," I said, squeezing a dollop of gel onto my hands and rubbing it gently over her scruffy mound and stubbly labia.

It took me a good thirty minutes to finish shaving her, especially the super-sensitive area on the sides of her vulva and along her perineum between her pussy and her asshole. Although I was nervous about cutting her at various times, the act of shaving her most private regions with a sharp blade while I stared at her dripping pussy was a tremendous turn on. I could feel my own juices running down the insides of my thighs while I smiled at Hannah's inflamed clit and tumescent lips as I carefully trimmed her stubble.

When I finished, she picked up a hand-held mirror from the vanity table and angled it toward her snatch, admiring my handiwork.

"You did a good job, Slave," she smiled, rubbing her hand over her smooth-as-velvet skin. "There might be a little reward in this for you later if you continue to be a good girl. But first, there's one other grooming job I want you to attend to while you're down there."

Hannah fetched another bag of items from one of the drawers, then unzipped the bag and handed me a nail file.

"I haven't done my *nails* in a while either," she said. "I want you to file them down a quarter of an inch and make them just as smooth as my pussy."

I took one look at the length of her nails and furrowed my forehead.

"Have you got some clippers? It's going to take quite a while to sand them down that much–"

Hannah grabbed my wet hair and pulled my face up to meet her angry gaze.

"Remember who's in *charge* here," Hannah said. "I want you to take your time and do them the professional way. And don't talk back to your master like that. You've got to learn your position as my slave. Now get to work."

As I lifted one of Hannah's feet and began sanding her toenails with the nail file, I began to wonder if this whole dom and submissive thing was still a good idea. She seemed to be getting a little too seriously into the role. She was no longer the happy-go-lucky, always-joking-around best friend I remembered. I figured I'd entertain her with this little escapade for another couple of hours or so. Then I'd be happy to revert back to my usual role taking the lead in my sexual affairs.

But as I looked up at Hannah with doleful eyes, she peered down and winked at me with a lopsided smile.

I guess she's just getting into character, I thought. *Let's see how far she wants to take this thing. Maybe she's trying to teach me a lesson.*

As I caressed her soft feet, I glanced up at her newly shaven pussy and noticed a dribble of lubrication dripping out of her hole and down the crack of her ass. I peered back up at her and winked with my opposite eye.

Yin and Yang. Tops and bottoms. Domme and femme. Maybe this was the natural way of the world after all.

4

———

fter I finished Hannah's pedicure, she leaned over and towel-dried my hair then patted me down to remove the last vestiges of water remaining on my back. Then she held out her hand and raised me off my knees, leading me toward the bedroom. When we got to her large four-poster bed, we stopped and I looked at her expectantly, hoping we'd finally have a chance to connect and have sex like we used to. Instead, she just looked at me blankly then pushed me backwards over the foot of the bed, where I toppled onto her mattress face up with my legs spread apart.

"Perfect," she said. "Stay in that position while I collect a few things for our next act."

Hannah fished through her chest of drawers, then returned with a jumble of scarves, placing them on the bed beside me.

"Mmm," I said, smiling at her with a raised eyebrow. "Are you going to blindfold me?"

"No," she said. "But you won't be needing your eyes for

this next thing I have in mind. Or your *hands*, for that matter."

Hannah picked up one of the scarves and wound it around my right wrist, then she pulled my arm up to the corner of the bed near the headboard and tied the loose ends around one of the posts, double-tying the knot firmly. Then she went around to the other side of the bed and repeated the procedure, tying my other hand to the other post. As she walked down toward the foot of the bed, she looked at me with a sly smile then she grasped my two feet and pulled me forcefully toward her, stretching my arms out straight.

"Ow!" I said, more playfully than actually hurting in pain. "There's no need to be so rough with me."

"I'm sorry if I hurt your feelings," Hannah smirked. "Remember, this whole thing was *your* idea. You can stop it at any time you want by saying the magic word."

"You mean 'stop', or 'I don't want to play anymore'?"

"Either of those will do. You're always in charge of what happens to your body."

I peered up at her with a little girl pout, then smiled.

"No," I said. "I don't want you to stop. I just want you to remember who you're playing with here. Someday the tables might be turned around the other way."

"Oh, I *definitely* know what I'm playing with," Hannah said as she tied my two feet to the bottom bedposts, admiring my naked body spread-eagled on top of her mattress. "And I plan to take maximum advantage of it while I have the chance."

She crawled up onto the mattress from the base of the bed and kneeled between my legs, running her eyes up and down my figure.

"You look absolutely delectable in this position, Jade," she said, her eyes widening at the prospect of ravishing me in my helpless state. "I'm going to take my time getting off this time while you caress and nibble every part of my body."

"That might be kind of hard to do in my current predicament," I said, thrashing my hands and feet to remind her of my limited mobility.

"That's okay," she said. "You're not going to need any of those extra appendages with what I'm planning to do to you. Everything except your *mouth*, that is. I have special plans for *that* part of your anatomy."

"Mmm," I purred, happy to have a chance to lick her body again. "Well then, scooch right on up here. I'll be happy to eat your pussy while you sit on my face–"

"All in good time, my dear," she said. "But first, there's a few *other* parts of your body I'd like to play with."

Hannah lifted one of her knees and straddled my left thigh, then lowered her pussy on top of my warm skin. I could feel her wetness coating my leg as she began to rock her hips against my flexing upper thigh muscle.

"Your skin feels so soft, Jade," she said, temporarily dispensing with the pejorative term she'd used for me previously. "You've done a nice job shaving my peachka nice and smooth. You feel exquisite against my skin."

"As do you, Han–I mean *Master*," I said. "I can feel your juices coating my leg."

"Yes," Hannah nodded. "I plan on leaving my mark all over you before I'm finished with you."

"Fuck, yes," I said, lifting my hips off the mattress, begging her to move her body closer to my aching snatch.

Hannah looked down at my bald pussy and licked her

lips. Then she slowly dragged her dripping crotch over the length of my upper thigh, pausing when she reaching my apex. I could feel the warmth of her left thigh pressing up against my vulva, and I humped my hips, vainly trying to gain the necessary friction to stimulate my clit.

Noticing the desperation in my eyes, she lifted herself off me temporarily, then repositioned herself straddling my upper pelvis with her two legs. Then she lowered her wet pussy onto the top of my mound and proceeded to grind her clit against my hard pubic bone. She let out a deep guttural moan and I tried to angle my hips upward to gain traction on my own burning gland, but instead she pressed me back down onto the mattress, careful to position her pussy just out of reach of my tingling gland.

"You're *evil*, you know that?" I hissed, giving her a death stare.

"It's all part of the role, baby," she smiled. "You wanted to be the slave. It's your job to give *me* pleasure, not the other way around."

"*Fine*," I huffed. "I'm enjoying the show plenty enough as it is. In fact, I could probably get off just watching you rub your pussy against my muff."

"I suppose you could," Hannah said, knowing full well as a sex therapist about neurological phenomenon of referred pleasure and pain. "I guess we'll just have to find another way to stimulate my pussy then."

Hannah wiggled her body up higher on my torso, shifting her weight from one knee to the other until she reached my tits, which by now were swollen and distended from the intense stimulation I was experiencing. Then she lowered her dripping pussy onto one of my erect teats and proceeded to fuck my little phallus between her slippery labia.

"Oh my God," I hummed. "That feels incredible. Fuck my tit with your pretty pussy, Hannah."

"*Who?*" she said, glaring at me indignantly.

"I mean *Master*. Fuck me with your smooth pussy, Master. I want to watch you cum all over my big tits."

"I'd love to accommodate you, my dear," she smiled. "But I have other plans for cumming all over you."

She suddenly lifted herself up and turned her body around with her ass toward my head then slowly inched her gaping hole up toward my face.

"Yes," I panted. "Sit on my face. I want to suck on that nicely shaved pussy and flick my tongue all over that big bean."

"I think we can manage that," Hannah said, lowering her glistening crotch onto my eagerly awaiting mouth.

When I felt her slippery folds press against my face, I lapped up her juices like a hungry puppy dog. She pressed her pelvis hard against my jaw, and I could feel her hard button rubbing against the top row of my teeth. I spread my lips to give her maximum friction against the hard surface, and she began to rock her hips rapidly forward and back. The crack of her ass kept rubbing against my nose, but this only added to the excitement of the situation, especially as I inhaled the sweet smell of the jasmine still lingering on her skin.

While Hannah picked up the pace of her rocking and grinding, she bent forward and began licking my tits, wildly rimming my tingling nipples with her slathering tongue. As I watched her pretty pucker flexing inches away from my wide eyes, I began to feel the familiar pangs of an orgasm building up inside me. But once again, just as I was about to reach the crest of my pleasure, she lifted herself off me, holding her body inches away from my flapping tongue desperately trying to reach her inflamed clit.

"What the fuck, Hannah–" I started to object.

But I didn't have a chance to finish my complaint as she tilted her hips forward, planting her ass directly over my lips.

"Shut up and lick my asshole, Slave," she huffed. "There's plenty of *other* ways we can put that talented tongue to work."

At first, I was surprised by the temerity of Hannah's bold move, but as she began to spread her legs further apart and wiggle her ass on my face, I quickly forgot about what part of her body I was licking and began munching on her anus with unremitted abandon. There was no trace of any unpleasant smell or taste, only the warm feeling of her soft flesh in my mouth and the sweet smell of the jasmine body wash.

As Hannah began to moan in delight above me, I extended my tongue and probed her hole, rolling it around the edges and washing it with my warm saliva. I'd never licked a woman's asshole before, but I knew that it was a highly erogenous zone and that it was everyone's fantasy. And from the sound of Hannah's rapidly escalating whimpers and moans above me, it was obvious this was one of *Hannah's* too.

As she began to shake her hips more rapidly over my face and press her weight down harder onto my face, I could see her butt cheeks beginning to quiver in a state of imminent climax. When her orgasm finally hit her, Hannah wailed at the top of her lungs as her whole body shook like she was having an epileptic seizure. When I felt her sphincter pulsing in my mouth, I couldn't hold back any longer and I raised my hips high off the mattress, gushing like a faucet from my own powerful orgasm taking hold of me. For what seemed like an eternity, the two of us swiveled our hips wildly, locked in the most powerful orgasm either one of us had experienced in a long time.

Referred pleasure indeed, I thought as my orgasm slowly began to ebb. *Maybe I should try this role-play stuff more often.*

5

———

When Hannah finally stopped shaking over top of my face, she lifted herself up and flopped down on the mattress beside me, breathing heavily.

"Holy *fuck*," I said. "Was that just me, or was that the most erotic, powerful orgasm I've had in a long time?"

"No," she panted. "You aren't kidding. I haven't cum that hard, since, well, the *last* time I was with you."

"Who knew the anus could be such a pleasure receptor?" I said, licking my tongue over my mouth to taste the remnants of her scent still on my lips.

"I guess the gay guys are on to something after all," she nodded.

I turned my head toward her and peered at her with a sly smile.

"That's the *real* reason you wanted me to wash you down there, isn't it? You had this whole thing planned right from the beginning."

"Maybe, she smirked. But the pussy shave and pedicure

also helped to put me in the mood. I almost came watching you stare at my pussy while you filed my nails."

"You're such a bitch," I said, giving her a gentle nudge with my elbow.

"That's bitch-*Master*, to you," she grinned back at me.

"Yes Master," I nodded obsequiously. "So what now? Are you going to untie me and let me properly satisfy myself now? If I don't touch my clit soon, I'm going to explode."

"Maybe in a little while," Hannah said, giving me a devilish smile. "There's one last thing I wanted to do to you before we end this little submissive and dom thing."

"I can't imagine what else you could do to me that could be more defiling than rubbing your asshole into my face while I'm helplessly tied up."

"Oh, you have *no* idea," she said, getting up off the bed and heading back to her chest of drawers, where she retrieved a huge pink strap-on dildo.

"No *way*!" I said, shaking my head. "You weren't thinking of fucking me up the *ass* with that thing!?"

"Probably not," she smirked. "But I *do* like the idea of fucking you from behind with it."

Hannah placed the dildo on the bed and slowly untied each of my hands from the bedposts. Then she flipped me over and retied my hands in the same position, this time with me facing down onto the mattress.

"Holy shit, Hannah," I said. "Now I'm even more vulnerable than before. You can pretty much do whatever you want to me in this position."

"That's exactly the idea," she said, slowly strapping on the silicon dildo like she was a cowboy preparing for a gunslinging contest.

"Be careful with that thing," I said as she approached the side of the bed, estimating the length of the phallus at a good eight inches. "You could take someone's eye out with that thing if you're not too careful."

"Oh, don't worry," Hannah smiled. "I don't plan on going anywhere near your *face* with my pretty little cock. I've got some other plans for it. Now I'm *really* going to show you what it means to be a dom and a submissive."

Hannah hopped up on the bed straddling my hips and positioned her crotch directly above my bare ass cheeks. Then she rocked her hips up and down overtop of me, causing the flexible appendage attached to her harness to slap loudly against my buttocks.

"You said you wanted something to touch your pussy," she said. "Well get ready, because you're about to have the ride of your life."

"Yes, Master," I whinnied, tilting my ass up as much as my restraints allowed to give her freer access to my pussy.

For a long moment, Hannah paused inches above my ass with her weapon, and for a second I thought she was contemplating fucking me up the ass with it. But when I felt her grab the end of the dildo and swipe it gently up and down my quivering slit, I moaned in anticipation of her filling my aching cunt.

"Fuck me with your big dick, Master," I pleaded. "I need you to fill me up with your organ. I want to feel you inside me."

"Oh yes," Hannah grunted, positioning the tip of the phallus at the entrance to my dripping hole.

She pushed it in an inch or two, then paused for a moment before plunging it all the way inside my tight snatch.

"Uhn!" I grunted, feeling the probe pressing against the end of my cavity.

"Oh *God*, Hannah," I said, momentarily dispensing with

the proper terms I was supposed to use in our little game of top and bottom. "Fuck me with that thing like there's no tomorrow."

"Damn *straight*, girl," Hannah hissed, equally lost in the moment.

As she lowered her body onto my back, I felt her cool tits rubbing against my shoulder blades while she began to pound her hips forcefully against my buttocks. With each thrust, I clenched my cheeks, reveling in the feeling of her hard mound pressing up against me. She was fucking me hard and deep enough that I could feel the base of the dildo ramming against my tingling clit, and I tilted my hips up a degree or two higher to generate more friction.

It didn't take long for the feelings of another powerful orgasm to well up inside me, and as we both slapped our hips together like two bucking broncos, our combined cries of ecstasy escalated in likewise fashion. At the crest of my pleasure, I cried out to Hannah to signal that I was about to come.

"I'm going to cum, Han. I'm going to cum hard all over your big cock. Ram that monster inside me while I gush all over you pussy."

"*Fuck* yes," Hannah grunted, pressing her hips hard against my ass in one final forceful thrust as her tits quivered against my back at the beginning of another strong orgasm.

When I felt her cumming on top of me, I couldn't hold back and longer and I screamed at the top of my lungs as my entire vulva began flexing and clamping in a series of powerful contractions while the built-up fluid inside my pussy began spraying out the sides of our tight connection all over Hannah's buckling thighs behind the leather of her strap-on harness.

When we both finally stopped cumming after waking up the entire neighborhood, Hannah collapsed on top of my back with the dildo still inserted deep inside me, resting her head softly against my throbbing heart. Even though she had me in the most compromised possible submissive and dominant position possible at this moment, I could feel the love and tenderness emanating from her body as she wrapped her arms tenderly around me, softly caressing the sides of my breasts.

6

———

Hannah pulled the dildo out of me, then we cuddled for a while and fell asleep atop her mattress for a couple of hours. When I woke up, I heard her foraging around in the kitchen and I went downstairs to see what she was up to. When I saw that she was preparing a pasta salad, I peered up at her with a quizzical expression.

"I thought your *slave* was supposed to do all the domestic work," I joked. "Shouldn't *I* be the one getting dinner ready?"

She turned toward me and smiled.

"I thought maybe you'd like to switch roles for a while," she said. "Aren't you growing tired of being the submissive one yet?"

"Not really," I said with a sheepish grin. "After that last experience, I'm kind of getting into it. It's kind of fun being the bottom for a change."

"Just how far do you want to go with this thing?" she said, spooning some of the salad into a bowl and sliding it across the kitchen island toward me.

"*You're* the one in charge here," I said. "Use your imagination. Surely there must be a few *other* ways you can think of to use and abuse me."

Hannah pulled up a chair beside me and sat down to eat her salad as her eyes flitted around trying to think of what to do next. After a few minutes, she peered up at me with a mischievous smile on her face.

"*What?*" I said. "What are you dreaming up now?"

"It seems to me that the obvious next step in your evolution as a slave is to test the waters with a few *other* players. How would you feel about my taking you to a lesbian bar?"

"That doesn't sound like too much of a stretch," I said. "It's not like I haven't picked up a girl in a bar before..."

"Not the kind of bar *I* have in mind. It's pretty hard-core. Plus, I have an idea how we could make it a little more interesting."

"Oh?" I said. "Do tell."

"I was thinking maybe we could dress you up in a provocative costume, something more befitting of your role as a slave. Then we could *really* test how strong this dominant-submissive impulse is in a natural setting."

"What, you mean like in some kind of tight leather outfit or something?"

"Something like that," Hannah smiled. "Why don't we go to our friend Cheryl's sex shop and try a few things on? She's got some pretty wild outfits in the back."

"Okay," I said, feeling my panties beginning to dampen at the idea of parading myself around a lesbian bar dressed up in an sexy outfit.

After dinner, Hannah and I drove to Cheryl's Babeland store on Broadway, where she escorted us to a fitting room in the back of the store. After talking with Cheryl about what we had in mind, she disappeared into the back and brought out a few outfits for me to try on. The first few garments involved the predictable see-through lingerie sets and skimpy schoolgirl costumes, but when she brought us a full-length vinyl body suit with strategic hole placements, both of our eyes widened in excitement. Decorated with metal studs and large fabric cut-outs for the breasts, buttocks and crotch area, it left little to the imagination.

After I tried it on, Hannah's eyes opened as wide as saucers while she nodded at me with a huge grin on her face. Somehow, wearing this full-length shiny body suit made me feel even *more* naked by drawing attention to my private areas.

"Holy shit," she said, admiring me in the full-length dressing room mirror. "That is one shit-hot, smoking outfit."

"You can't possibly imagine me walking into a *public setting* wearing this thing?" I said, shaking my head as I turned my body around to examine just how revealing it was on both sides of my body.

"Um, actually," she smiled. "I can. Can you imagine the kind of interest you'll generate walking into a lesbian bar dressed up like that? Talk about a *chick magnet*. You'd have every butch-dyke hitting on you in no time."

"Not to mention most of the *other* girls in the bar," Cheryl nodded, coming into the dressing room to inspect my outfit. "But if you *really* want to attract the dommes and take your role-playing to the next level, I have one *other* accessory that'll finish this look off perfectly."

She disappeared back into the store, then returned with a studded leather collar and a long black leash.

"If you wore this with Hannah leading you on a tether, you'd leave zero doubt as to your position in the pecking order."

I paused for a moment, then looked at the two of them with an incredulous expression.

"Are you *kidding* me?" I said. "You think it'll be sexy leading me around like a dog on a *leash*?!"

"Well, you *did* say you wanted to see how far we could take this," Hannah smiled. "This would be pretty much taking it to the maximum degree."

"I've never really been in a lesbian bar before," I said. "What if everybody just wants to paw and molest me when they see me in this thing? Are you going to protect me if things get a little out of control?"

"Of course," Hannah said. "You're still my best friend. I wouldn't let anything happen to you that you didn't feel comfortable doing. But you shouldn't close your mind too much about exploring the possibilities with this scenario. You might actually *enjoy* the kind of attention you're likely to attract from certain members of the lesbian subculture.

"Just how dark does it *get* in these kinds of bars?" I said, peering at the bright overhead lights above me in the dressing room. "I'm going to feel pretty self-conscious if they can see my exposed body as easily as you can in here."

"It's a lot darker than *this*, believe me," Hannah said. "It *is* a pick-up bar, after all. There'll be a lot of extra-curricular activity going on in the corners. Don't worry–you won't be the *only* one attracting the attention of the circling wolves."

"Okay," I said, beginning to relax. "I'm willing to give it a try at least this once. I mean, how bad can it be, right? I'm the one who's ultimately in charge of what happens to my body."

"Exactly," Hannah said, turning her wrist to peer at her watch. "Come on. Let's get you home and lolled up to make you as irresistible as possible. I'm just as excited as you to witness the sexual dynamic in this situation.

After we drove back to Hannah's place, she had me sit down at her make-up table while she fussed over my mascara, eyebrows, and lipstick. After we were all done, we finished off the ensemble with a pair of six-inch-high stilettos, which I thought made me look even *more* like a cheap hooker.

"You're certainly not going to have any trouble attracting every red-blooded lesbian alpha in the room tonight," Hannah said, licking her lips at me. "I'd jump you *myself* right now if you weren't already bound up in that skin-tight costume."

I looked at Hannah with a raised eyebrow and smiled.

"There's still plenty of openings for you to have your way with me. Do you want to have another go with your big purple dildo?"

"Maybe later," Hannah chuckled. "Right now, I'm more excited to see how all the *other* lesbian women react to you. Let's go–it's getting close to prime time."

H annah and I drove over to the East side where we pulled into a large parking lot next to an industrial building painted in all black. A small neon sign hung over the entrance door flashing *Sappho* in pink letters. I could see a small group of women dressed up in torn jeans and spiky colored hair loitering near the door smoking cigarettes. They looked at our car when we pulled up, then resumed talking amongst themselves.

"Are you sure this is a good idea?" I said, looking at the bare-armed, tattooed girls standing by the door.

"Of course," Hannah said. "It'll be fun. Just lose yourself in the role, and see how it plays out. If you're not digging it, let me know and we can take off whenever you've had enough."

"Okay," I said, wondering what the hell I'd gotten myself into.

Hannah fished around in her purse then pulled out the leather collar and attached it around my neck, snapping on the leather leash and opening her door.

"You sit tight while I come around the other side to get you. If we're going to do this, we might as well play the roles to the full extent for the maximum effect."

"Yes, Master," I said, smiling at her with an obedient expression.

Hannah walked around to the other side of the car, then opened my door and picked up the leash, pulling me gently out of the car. When she led me around the back of the car and the women by the door caught sight of my outfit with Hannah leading me by the leash, everybody stopped talking and stared at me dumbfounded. Hannah simply pretended like everything was normal and walked nonchalantly past the crowd, nodding to a doorman who waved us past the door into the dark and noisy club.

When we entered the main room, there was a female impersonator singing a song on stage with a group of women dancing in the corner. As we headed over to the bar, all the girls milling nearby turned to look at the two of us, running their eyes up and down my body and staring at my exposed skin, which flashed like beacons under the overhead strobe light next to my blacked-out costume in the dark and musky room.

When we finally got to the bar, I tried to position myself in such a way to show the minimum amount of skin, but no matter which way I turned, I was either showing my bare-assed buttocks or exposed breasts and crotch.

"Jesus, Hannah," I said, cozying up to her as close as possible, trying to gain a modicum of cover. "This is even worse than I imagined. My exposed skin looks like its coated with fluorescent *paint* in this place. And everybody is staring at me!"

"I know," she smiled, motioning for the bartender to bring us some drinks. "Isn't it great? Don't you feel sexy dressed up showing off your best assets? If you wanted to play the submissive, this is your chance to test it on the ultimate stage. Just relax and enjoy all the attention. We've got the whole night ahead of us."

When the bartender arrived, Hannah ordered two mai tais and when he placed them on the counter in front of us, I grabbed one of the glasses, taking healthy gulp of the liquid courage.

"Just be cool, girl," Hannah said, pulling gently on my leash while wrapping her hand around the other end resting on the bar. "I got you. I mean, I really *got* you. No one's going to do anything either one of us wants them to do to you as long as they see who owns you."

"Okay," I said, beginning to feel the tension in my body relax as I shifted my weight slightly back from the bar. After a few minutes, a burly girl with a barbell stud in her lower lip approached the two of us, resting a heavily tattooed arm on the bar counter next to me.

"What's up, girl?" she said, glancing down at my protruding tits, pinched even tighter by the constricting black vinyl fabric. "That's quite a hot costume you're wearing."

"Um–thanks," I said, shifting my weight defensively to my other leg closest to Hannah.

"So what's your story?" she said, placing her other hand on my exposed ass while caressing my bare buttocks. "Are you two looking for a little fun, or is this a closed-loop kind of relationship?"

"That depends on what kind of mood my girl is in," Hannah said, eyeing the woman suspiciously while she looked down at her molesting hand disapprovingly. "She's *my* girl, but I might be interested in sharing the spoils if the mood strikes. What do you say, Jade? Do you want to find a private corner and explore some of the boundaries?"

I shifted my weight closer to Hannah while rubbing my body against her, signaling my interest in remaining fully under her control for the time being.

"I'm pretty happy staying with you right now, Master," I said, rubbing my ass against her hip to demonstrate my subordination.

"You heard the girl, *bitch*," Hannah said, swiping the woman's hand away from my ass. "Take your hands off her. This one's *mine*. Go find somebody else to play with."

"Whatever," the girl said, backing away from the bar and uttering a few curse words as she disappeared into the crowd.

"Well, I guess that's *one* way to attract the dominant wolves in the pack," I sighed, turning to take another gulp of my drink.

"You're not feeling the sexual energy so far?" she said, peering around at the other people in the bar.

"Not with *that* one at least," I said. "She was coming on a little too strong. Plus, she wasn't really my type. I don't mind mixing it up with a strong-minded woman, maybe just someone a little hotter, you know?"

"Yeah," Hannah nodded. "I get your drift."

She ordered another round of drinks, then yanked me gently by my harness, leading me across the room to a padded lounge in the corner of the bar where a group of attractive women were chatting amongst themselves and cheering while they watched the performer on the stage. As we approached their table, Hannah motioned with her head to gain their attention momentarily.

"Have you got room for two more?" she said. "We could use a more comfortable spot to sit down, and you girls look like you're up for a little fun."

"Absolutely, one of the women with shorter hair said, pushing the rest of the girls over to make room for us in the middle of the circular seat cushion. "Feel free to get nice and cozy right here between the group of us. It's got the best view of the stage."

Hannah squeezed past the girls on one side of settee, pulling me by the leash as I followed her submissively, taking a spot framed by the first girl and another one with tattooed arms beside me.

"I haven't seen you two in here before," the lead girl sitting next to Hannah said. "Were you just looking to take in the show, or were you looking for a *different* kind of action?"

"We're just kind of playing it as it goes," Hannah said, glancing over at the performer on the stage vamping it up as she sang the Melissa Etheridge anthem Come to my Window. "She's pretty good. She kind of even *looks* a bit like Melissa Etheridge."

"That's the whole idea," the girl said, holding her hands over her crotch like she was grabbing a cock. "But everybody knows she's got some *different* equipment to work with."

"Yeah, I can see that," Hannah said, noticing the singer's Adam's Apple bobbing up and down while she sang.

"Not like your *friend* here," the girl said, staring at my exposed tits poking out above the table. "She's got *all* the right equipment to work with."

Hannah peered over at me silently to see if I was receptive to the obvious advances of the girl, and I smiled at her blankly, taking another swig of my drink. The two alcoholic beverages were already making me a bit tipsy having only eaten a small salad all day, and I slumped back in the chair, resting my head against the padded backrest. Taking this as a signal of receptivity, the girl sitting next to me raised her glass off the table, rubbing it gently against my exposed nipples. I enjoyed the sensation of the cool surface against my skin, and I slunk further down in my chair, feeling my nipples harden from the combined stimulation of the chilly glass and the rest of the girls watching me from the other side of the table.

"Mmm," the girl next to me hummed, glancing over at Hannah. "I think she likes this. I bet she's a very attentive slave when you need her to be."

"When I *want* her to be," Hannah said, winking at me playfully.

"Oh yeah?" the girl said, reaching her other hand under the table. "What does she like to do? Or should I say, what is she best at *giving*?"

"She's good at *everything*, when she's in the right mood," Hannah smiled. "Am I right, Jade? You kind of *like* it when someone else is in charge, don't you?"

I nodded demurely as I felt the girl's warm hand caressing my bald pussy, running her fingers gently up and down my moistening slit. As her fingers danced over my clit, I couldn't help spreading my legs further apart, getting increasingly turned on by all the attraction around the table. It was kind of fun being the center of attention in our corner of the room, and I could feel my pussy getting wetter and wetter as the rest of the girls' eyes widened while they licked their lips as my seatmate played with my pussy.

After a few minutes of teasing me with her fingers, she

grew increasingly bold with her exploration, and when I began to rock my hips in appreciation of what she was doing, she suddenly thrust three fingers deep into my cunt and began ramming her hand hard against my crotch as she leaned over to suck on my nipples into her mouth. I could feel myself getting increasingly turned on by all the stimulation in the public setting, and as I began to moan softly and begin to gyrate in my seat, two of the girls on the other side of the booth ducked underneath the table and crawled toward me, licking and nibbling on the insides of my legs.

They pushed my knees further apart and when their mouths reached my now-dripping pussy, the girl next to me removed her fingers from my hole, allowing the other girls to lick and lap up my juices in a combined two-person assault on my snatch. When the girl beside me began to pinch one of my hardened nipples and flick her fingernail against the flexing teat, the girl sitting next to Hannah couldn't resist any longer and reached over in front of her, rolling my other nipple hard between her fingers. Without any sign of protest on my part, she crawled overtop of Hannah who saw that I was enjoying all the attention, then she straddled my hips facing toward me as she ground her hips into my hard mound.

At first, I enjoyed the combined attention of the swarming mob, but as they grew increasingly rough and bold with their exploration of my body, I began to tense up. While I enjoyed the stimulation from a sexual point of view, I was beginning to feel a bit claustrophobic in the tight confines of the cloistered booth, and I began to pull my thighs together to deter the two women under the table from taking any further liberties.

But instead of reading my signal to back off, they yanked my legs even wider apart while taking turns ramming their fingers into me and lapping up the juices coating the inside of my thighs. When the butchy girl on top of me began kissing down the side of my neck and biting the muscle on top of my shoulder hard enough to cause me pain, I started to push back, trying to signal that I was beginning to feel uncomfortable with how they were taking advantage of me.

But between the action of the girl on top of me pulling me hard against the back of the cushion with her outstretched arms and the girl next to me pinching my nipples tightly and the two girls under the table taking turns ramming their fingers into me up to their knuckles, I was began to panic, and I pushed back more forcefully against the woman pinning me to the cushion while trying to close my thighs against the combined strength of the two women under the table.

When Hannan saw the panic in my eyes and my desperate attempts to free myself from the combined press of the four women, she reached out to the girl sitting on top of me, temporarily pulling her shoulders away from my pinned body.

"I think my girl's had enough of your attention for the time being," she said. "Can't you read the signals? I think she wants you to back off."

"I haven't heard her say stop yet," the girl on top of me said, yanking her body back against my torso with her strong arms, pressing me tightly against the back of the cushion.

"What do you say, Jade?" Hannah said, looking at me to affirm her suspicions. "Have you had enough for now?"

"Yes," I said. "This getting to be a bit too much."

"You heard the girl," Hannah said, trying to pull the big girl's shoulders away from me.

"*Back off*, bitch," she said, swiping Hannah's hand away

forcefully. "*You're* the one that brought this slave into our booth. You can have her back when we're finished with her."

"I'm sorry but that doesn't work for me," Hannah said, suddenly grabbing the woman's hair with two hands and yanking her backwards toward the table. "You heard the lady. No means no."

With her nostrils flaring and her eyes filled with rage, she slammed the girl's head hard against the top of the wooden table, momentarily stunning her. Then Hannah stood up on the settee, kicking the woman's head sitting next to me, snapping it backwards. Then she scampered over the top of the table and pulled the woman onto the floor in one swift move, glaring at the rest of the women around the table. Then she grabbed my hand and pulled me off the bench, freeing me from the grasp of the other two women under the table.

"Anyone *else* want to see who's in charge here?" she glared at the rest of the stunned girls sitting around the table. "Come on, baby, let's get the fuck out of this dive. These aren't the kind of chicks that deserve your attention."

Hannah unclipped the leash from my collar and threw it on the floor, then threaded her arm between mine and pushed her way through the club until we spilled out the exit door, breathing in the fresh air from the parking lot.

"I'm sorry, Jade," she said, peering at me as she pushed my ruffled hair to one side. "I didn't know things were going to get that quickly out of control in there."

"Yeah," I said, shaking my head, still in shock. "I think I've had my fill of this whole dom and submissive thing. Although I gotta say, you really turned me on with that whole alpha-wolf, kick-ass performance in there. Where did *that* come from?"

"I just kind of lost control when I saw how they were

taking advantage of my best friend and starting to hurt you. I'd never stand by when I saw someone trying to do anything to you that you weren't enjoying."

"Thanks, hun," I said, throwing my arms around her. "Can we go home now and make love the way we used to? You know, when neither one of us is thinking about who's in charge or who's on the top or the bottom. I just want to make love like we're *equals* again."

"Absolutely," Hannah said. "I think I learned just as much from this little experiment as you. Ultimately, every successful relationship depends on mutual respect and consent. It's fine to play master and submissive every now and then, but only with the underpinnings of a real abiding love. Otherwise, it can quickly devolve into an unhealthy dynamic."

"I couldn't have said it better myself," I said, kissing her gently on the cheek. "Come on, there's someone *else* I feel like sharing the love with right now..."

Everybody's an exhibitionist in disguise...

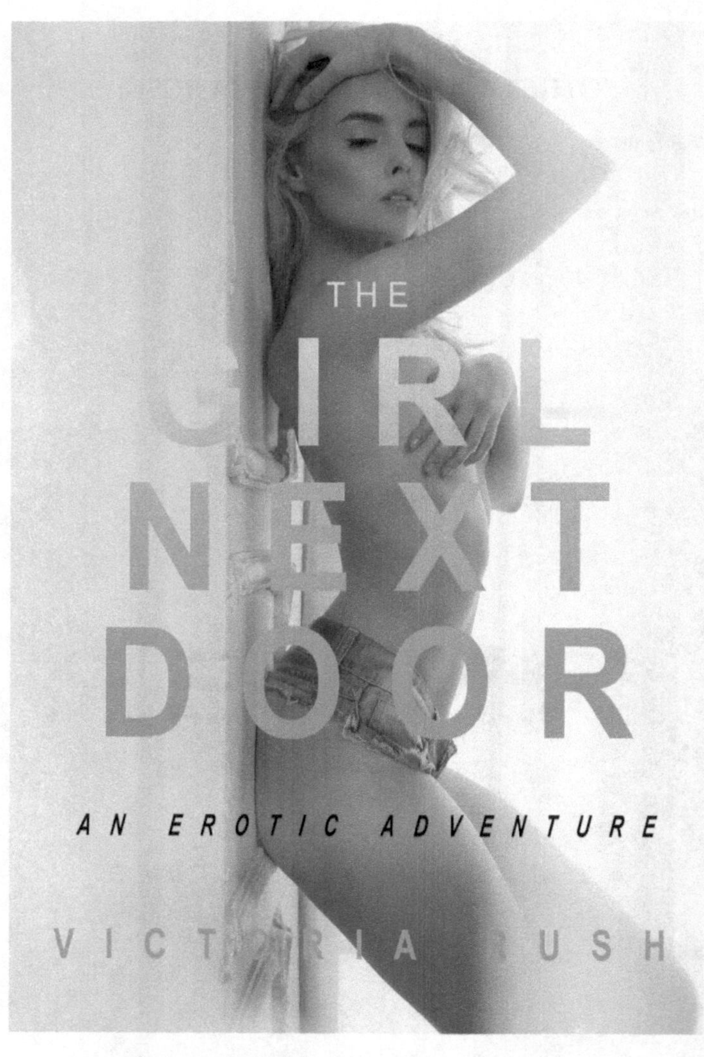

Spying on the neighbors just got a lot more interesting...

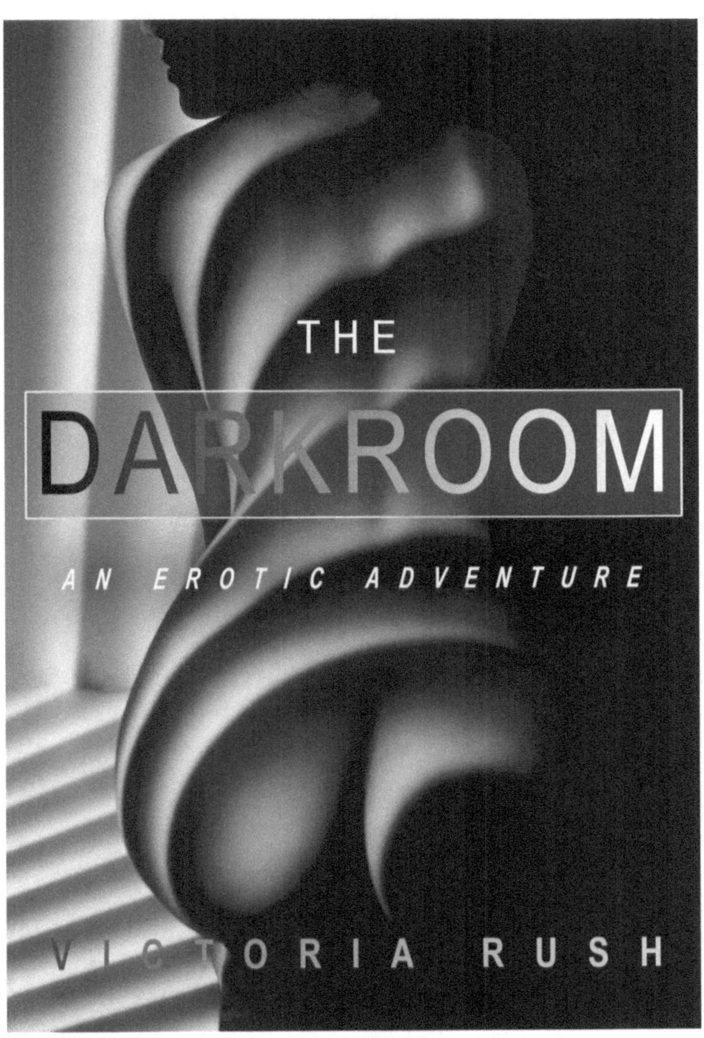

Everything's sexier in the dark...

Artificial intelligence never felt so real...

Books 6 - 10 in the bestselling series - now 60% off.

Sometime later, I heard a soft tap on my bedroom door. Not wanting to remove myself just yet from my cocoon of luxury, I called out to answer.

"Yes?"

"It's time for your massage," a woman's voice replied.

"Just one minute please."

I reluctantly stepped out of the bath and quickly toweled myself dry. I wrapped a large bath sheet around me, re-donned my mask, then opened the bedroom door.

A petite young Asian girl greeted me, wearing a kimono similar to mine and a crimson masquerade mask.

Apparently not everybody who works here always walks around stark naked.

The girl was utterly breathtaking. Long jet-black hair cascaded over high cheekbones past pouty lips, her delicate collarbones peeking from the top of her kimono. I could see her breasts and hips outlined by the tightly-wrapped kimono and suddenly wished that she too had come to my boudoir naked.

"My name is Jasmine," she said. "I'm your personal

masseuse and esthetician. Are you ready for your final preparation?

Just the thought of this beauty laying her tender hands on me sent a shiver down my spine.

"Definitely. Please come in. How would you like me to prepare?"

"Come with me, please."

Jasmine led me into the bathroom, where she nonchalantly removed her kimono and hung it behind the bathroom door.

Oh my God.

I didn't think anyone in this place could get more beautiful or sensuous. Jasmine had perfectly shaped B-cup breasts with a thin indentation running down the center of her perfectly toned stomach. Like everyone else in this place, her pubis was utterly bald and flawless. She barely looked eighteen and I was just about to ask her age, but she spoke first.

"If you'd like to remove your towel and lay face down on the table, we can get started. May I call you Jade?"

There was something about her confident manner and tone that belied her youthful appearance. I had no inhibitions whatsoever about displaying myself unclothed to this stranger.

"Yes, thank you, Jasmine." I unhooked my bath sheet and threw it against the side of the tub.

"Would you like me to drape your backside?" Jasmine asked.

"That won't be necessary," I quickly answered.

Jasmine walked over to the vanity counter and picked up two small bottles of oil resting under an orange radiant lamp. She brought them back to the massage table, opened one, and poured the oil into one cupped hand then rubbed her hands together. The scent of lavender wafted toward my nose.

I closed my eyes in anticipation of her touch. I'd had massages before, but nothing as sensuous and stimulating as this. When her hands touched the small of my back, I jerked reflexively from the sexual tension. My heart was beating a hundred miles an hour as I felt the blood coursing through my veins.

Jasmine must have sensed my nervous tension and began pressing her fingers more firmly into my back as she moved them slowly up each side of my spine. The warm oil allowed her hands to glide effortlessly across my skin. She used every surface of her hands to massage my muscles, expertly kneading my skin with her fingers and palm.

I began to relax as my muscles softened and surrendered to her touch. She sensuously massaged every part of my back, shoulders, and neck, applying just the right amount of pressure. Periodically, she would pour more warm oil on my lower back, dipping her hands in it to replenish the silky lubrication against my pliant skin.

Just as the sexual tension began to subside from the utter relaxation of the massage, Jasmine moved her hands down to my buttocks and began to caress them in soft circular motions. My glutes contracted involuntarily and I unconsciously pressed my mound into the firm padding of the table. Suddenly I was quickly reminded that a gorgeous young woman was caressing my naked body. She cupped each buttock between her hands as she massaged my ass tantalizingly, her little finger sliding slowly into the cleft just above my anus.

Periodically, I'd partially open one of my eyes with my head turned in her direction to look at her gorgeous body. My head was at the same level as her midsection, and my mouth watered as I watched her stomach muscles flex and her hips undulate with each movement of her hands. At times her pussy was almost right beside me and I wanted to reach out and run my own fingers up her soft legs.

I was in total heaven and getting wetter by the moment. Just when I thought I couldn't stand it anymore, she suddenly moved her hands down to my feet and began massaging her thumbs into my soles.

I'd always loved having my feet massaged, but nobody did it like Jasmine. She cradled my foot and used every part of her hands to massage and knead every surface from my heel to my toes. I didn't want her to stop, but there were other parts of my body that were screaming for attention.

As if reading my thoughts, she began moving her hands up toward my calf, using her thumbs to spread the muscle apart. She lingered almost as long on my calf as she had on my foot, rolling the ball of my calf between both of her hands, sliding her slick hands up and down erotically. I couldn't help imagining how she might use those same hands to massage a man's erect cock in a similar manner. My mind wandered again to what pleasures lay in wait for me over dinner.

After shifting her hands to my right leg and giving my other foot and calf similar attention, she placed each hand just behind my knees and began to slowly move them up towards my buttocks. Her thumbs pressed against my inner thighs as she glided tantalizingly close to my apex.

I rolled my legs outward in an invitation to move closer. My legs were parted enough that I was sure she could see my vulva from her vantage point behind me. In my highly aroused state, my lips were engorged and spread apart, revealing my moist and quivering opening.

But as much as I desperately wanted her to, Jasmine

never touched me there. She repeatedly slid her hands right up to the edge of my slit, pressing and rotating her thumbs on the fleshy meat of my upper thighs just below my aching pussy. I suppose this was part of her master plan—to tease me mercilessly and inflame my passions so I'd be ready for just about anything at the main event.

It was certainly working. After thirty minutes of Jasmine's ministrations, I was grinding my pussy into the table trying desperately to give my clit some needed direct stimulation.

Just when I thought I couldn't be teased any more tantalizingly, Jasmine opened one of the bottles of warm oil and poured it directly into the crack of my ass. She paused as the fluid flowed down and directly over my parted lips. I almost came from the gentle movement of the warm liquid as it trickled across the folds of my labia, channeled toward the junction where they joined together at my clit. I shuddered in pleasure at the feeling, even if it was only the subtlest of touch.

Jasmine suddenly interrupted my thoughts.

"Would you like to turn over now?"

It was the first time she had spoken directly to me since the massage started, and it surprised me in my catatonic, pre-orgasmic state. I practically flipped over like a fish out of water and spread my legs expectantly. Finally, I'd get some relief. Surely, she couldn't leave me hanging like this.

"It's time for your final grooming," she said. "I'll need you to part your legs a bit further to provide full access."

Grooming? I knew this was part of the process, but somehow it didn't seem fair to transition at this precise moment. At least I'd be able to stay on the comfortable massage table instead of the clinical vinyl chairs used by my regular esthetician.

Jasmine walked over to another cabinet by the makeup table and withdrew a leather bag from one of the drawers, then brought it back to the table. She reached into the bag and pulled out a cordless hair trimmer.

"Do you have a preference regarding your appearance?" she asked. "Do you prefer natural, neatly trimmed, or bare?"

I knew she was referring to my pubic hair, which I generally kept neatly trimmed. I'd always thought going fully bald was unnatural and unseemly, catering to men's prurient fantasies of fucking young schoolgirls. But in this situation, it seemed entirely appropriate, like I was stripping away all my camouflage and armor.

If tonight was all about being watched, I might as well bare myself in every sense of the word and truly let my inhibitions go. I began to fantasize about rubbing my bare pussy against Jasmine's while she poured warm oil between us. The more work she had to do on me, the more chance I'd have to make this last and hopefully get off.

I didn't hesitate. "Bare, thank you."

"As you wish," she said. "I'll remove the long hairs first with the trimmer, then shave you smooth with a razor."

No waxing? This was different. I was relieved to not have to bear the painful and violent trial of having my hairs ripped out en masse. Although shaving down there was always a scary proposition, I felt safe in the capable and practiced hands of this beautiful esthetician.

Jasmine nodded, then flipped a switch on the trimmer. The device buzzed softly as she placed it gently on my mound. I had only a light dusting of fur and it didn't take long for her to remove it with a few short strokes over my pubis. I shuddered as the vibrations penetrated deep into my core. If she had placed the flat head on my clitoris, I would have popped off in a millisecond. Instead, she turned the trimmer face-down and gently swiped the vibrating teeth against the sides of my vulva, sensuously separating my labia with her hands as she moved the device between my legs to trim the hairs on the inside and outside of my labia.

It was an insanely titillating feeling, but just clinical enough to bring me down from my plateau and shift my focus. My mind wandered to the upcoming feast, and I contemplated what surprises lay in wait at the main event. The hostesses had suggested there would be 'contact' of some sort during the meal, and I was intrigued exactly who and how it would be administered. The idea of being fully bald, cleansed, and thoroughly stimulated going into the event was an incredible rush.

Jasmine continued with the trimmer all the way down my perineum to my anus, barely touching me with the trimmer so as not to pinch any delicate tissues. Apparently there were no parts of my erogenous zone that would remain untouched, now—and perhaps later.

She turned off the trimmer and placed it at the foot of the table. Then she took a bottle of gel from the bag and spread the gel on her hands. Using both hands, she spread it gently between my legs, starting on my mound all the way down to my rosebud.

My body almost levitated above the table as Jasmine finally laid her hands directly on my clitoris. The gel had a mild stinging quality that added to the stimulating sensation. If this was meant to excite my follicles in preparation for the shave, it wasn't the only feature of my anatomy that it made erect. I could feel the hood of my clitoris retract as my button filled with blood and began to push outward. Suddenly, I was fully stimulated again and lusting for Jasmine's touch. I fantasized about her bending down and taking my swollen nub between her puffy lips and letting me come in her mouth.

Unfortunately, my satisfaction would have to wait a little longer. Instead, Jasmine reached into her bag and pulled out a straight-edge razor. In anyone else's hands, it might look threatening, especially in my prostrated and vulnerable position. But something about the way she delicately and sensuously opened the jackknifed tool instantly evaporated my fears. I could see how this type of razor would in fact give her better control safely cutting my stubs instead of the usual ladies plastic razor.

With her right hand, Jasmine gently laid the razor on its flat edge at the top of my mound, while she gently pulled my skin upwards with her other hand. Then she slowly turned the sharp edge perpendicular to my skin and began softly scraping the razor downwards. I could hear the bristling sound as the razor edge removed my nubs right down to the follicles. She repeated the pattern in one inch wide swipes on one side then the other of my pubis, being ever-so-careful to stop just where my clitoris lay quivering in a mixture of fear and excitement. There was something about the utter vulnerability of the procedure that made it the most erotic experience I'd ever had.

Jasmine used the same deft touch as she moved down my vulva and perineum, scraping the vestiges of stray hairs away with gentle swipes of the long blade, while sensuously separating my folds and flesh with her other hand. She took extra time and care around my anus and clit, using the gentlest and slowest motion I've ever felt someone apply to my body. The combination of fright and titillation as she probed my most sensitive body parts created a river of sensuous fluids running down my vulva. By this time, no shaving gel was necessary to provide a smooth gliding surface for the knife.

When she was finished, Jasmine retrieved a fresh wash towel from beside the sink and held it under the warm water faucet then twisted the excess water into the basin. She returned to the table and placed it over my splayed legs then gently cleansed the excess moisture and remaining shaving gel with gentle massaging movements of her hands. The warm, moist towel felt exquisite against my newly shaved skin. Jasmine's hands now felt comforting between my legs rather than erotic.

She had taken me on an incredibly sensuous erotic arc, right to the edge of ecstasy and back, to a quiet relaxed place. I exhaled fully and completely for the first time in almost an hour.

Jasmine removed the towel from between my legs and held up a large hand mirror at a forty-five degree angle toward me.

"What do you think?" she asked.

I tilted my head up and studied her masterpiece. Far from the usual red and swollen vulva that I typically experienced after the violent waxing with my regular esthetician, I'd never seen my pussy look so beautiful. Utterly bereft of any hair, my entire perineum from my pubic mound to my anus was totally bald, pink—and gorgeous. I just stared at my beautiful pussy, utterly transfixed by the transformation.

"You have to *feel* it to really appreciate how beautiful you are, Jade," Jasmine purred.

I moved my right hand down, running my fingers along the edges of my pussy. I gasped from a feeling I'd never felt before. It felt smooth as silk: no bumps or blemishes or cuts or bruises. It was almost as if I was feeling somebody else— somebody I'd never felt before. I couldn't stop my left hand joining the other in rubbing and caressing my sensitive organs.

Jasmine lowered the mirror and smiled at me as I felt the moisture begin to accumulate between my legs again.

"It's almost time for your dinner appointment," she said. "Why don't you save the best for last? I think you'll find plenty of ways to satisfy your appetite over the next couple of hours."

She lifted my kimono from the hook at the edge of the bathtub and held it open for me.

"I'll escort you downstairs now if you're ready. All you need to bring is your kimono and slippers—and your mask of course."

I sat up slowly and stepped off the massage table. Turning around, I held my arms out as Jasmine lifted one arm of the silk robe onto me then the other. Then she turned around to face me, wrapped the silk tie around me, and tied a single bow over my belly button. She retrieved my matching silk slippers and knelt down on one knee to gently lift my feet one at a time and place them softly inside. It took every ounce of my power not to grab her head and pull it into my pulsating pussy.

Jasmine stood up gracefully and smiled into my eyes.

"If you'll follow me, I'll escort you now to the fantasy feast."

She didn't bother putting her own robe on. Her tight little ass barely jiggled as she stepped smartly ahead of me. I wasn't sure if I'd have a chance to feel Jasmine's touch again before the evening was over, but for now I was in total bliss ogling her petite, curvaceous figure from behind...

Read More

ABOUT THE AUTHOR

If you would like to receive notification of new book(s) in Jade's Erotic Adventures, follow me at http://bookbub.com/authors/victoria-rush.

If you have a moment, please post a brief review on my Amazon book page at: viewbook.at/theslave . Even just a couple of sentences will help other readers find and enjoy this book as much as you hopefully did.

Follow, share, like, and comment at:

www.facebook.com/authorvictoriarush
www.pinterest.com/authorvictoriarush
www.twitter.com/authorvictoriarush
authorvictoriarush@outlook.com

Hope to see you again soon!